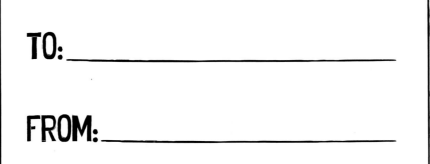

TO:_____

FROM:_____

DARE
TO DREAM
BIG

First published in the United States in 2020 by Sourcebooks
Text © 2019, 2020 by Lorna Gutierrez
Cover images and illustrations © 2019, 2020 by Polly Noakes
Cover and internal design © 2020 by Sourcebooks

Sourcebooks and the colophon are registered trademarks of Sourcebooks.

Ink and watercolor were used to create the full-color art.

Published by Sourcebooks Jabberwocky, an imprint of Sourcebooks Kids
P.O. Box 4410, Naperville, Illinois 60567-4410
(630) 961-3900
sourcebookskids.com

Originally published in 2019 in the UK as DARE by Tiny Owl Publishing, London.

Library of Congress Cataloging-in-Publication Data is on file with the publisher.

Source of Production: Leo Paper, Heshan City, Guangdong Province, China
Date of Production: September 2019
Run Number: 5016170

Printed and bound in China.
LEO 10 9 8 7 6 5 4 3 2 1

DARE

TO DREAM

BIG

WORDS BY **LORNA GUTIERREZ**

PICTURES BY **POLLY NOAKES**

sourcebooks
jabberwocky

Dare to *dream*.

Dare to *fly higher*.

Dare to trust...

Dare to inspire!

Dare to do what hasn't been done.

Dare to be second to none.

Dare to see
*when others
don't...*

Dare to speak

when others won't.

Dare to reach out

*and take
a chance.*

Dare to sing,
dare to dance.

Dare to have
a hand to lend.

Dare to be your own best friend.

Dare
to enjoy
a silent
night.

Dare to be who you **truly are**.

A light
in the dark.

Be you...

a star!